Spot the Shape

Shapes in Sport

Rebecca Rissman

www.raintreepublishers.co.uk
Visit our website to find out more information about Raintree books.

To order:

☎ Phone 0845 6044371

▤ Fax +44 (0) 1865 312263

▣ Email myorders@capstonepub.co.uk

Customers from outside the UK please telephone +44 1865 312262

Edited by Rebecca Rissman, Charlotte Guillain and Catherine Veitch
Designed by Joanna Hinton-Malivoire
Picture research by Tracy Cummins and Heather Mauldin
Originated by Dot Gradations Ltd
Printed in China by South China Printing Company Ltd

ISBN 978 0 431 19292 5 (hardback)
13 12 11 10 09
10 9 8 7 6 5 4 3 2 1

ISBN 978 0 431 19298 7 (paperback)
14 13 12 11 10
10 9 8 7 6 5 4 3 2 1

British Library Cataloguing in Publication Data
Rissman, Rebecca
Shapes in sport. - (Acorn. Spot the shape)
516.1'5
A full catalogue record for this book is available from the British Library.

Acknowledgements
We would like to thank the following for permission to reproduce photographs: ©Alamy pp. **4** (Barrie Rokeach), **11** (SBP), **12** (SBP); ©Getty Images pp. **7** (David Madison), **8** (David Madison), **13** (Debra McClinton), **14** (Debra McClinton), **15** (Dugald Bremner), **16** (Dugald Bremner), **17** (Doug Pensinger), **18** (David Madison), **19** (Stockbyte), **20** (Stockbyte), **23** (Dugald Bremner); ©Jupiter Images pp. **9** (Corbis), **10** (Corbis); ©Shutterstock pp. **6** (Saniphoto), **21** (Jonathan Larsen).

Cover photograph of a football on a field reproduced with permission of ©Superstock/Corbis. Back cover photograph of a bicycle reproduced with permission of ©Getty Images (Stockbyte).

Every effort has been made to contact copyright holders of material reproduced in this book. Any omissions will be rectified in subsequent printings if notice is given to the publishers.

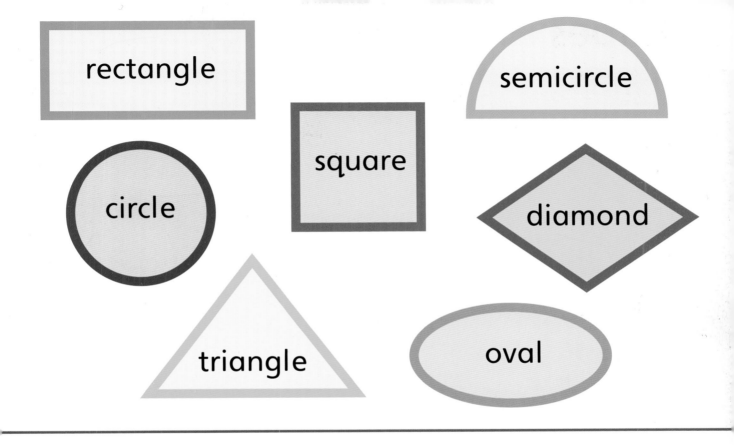

rectangle

semicircle

circle

square

diamond

triangle

oval

Each shape has a name.

Shapes in sport

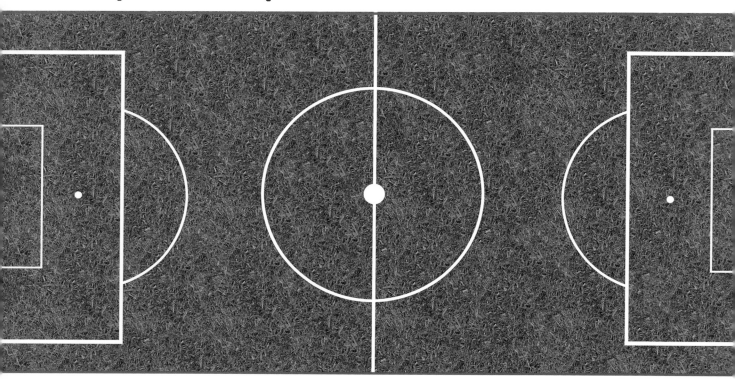

There are many shapes in sport.

What shapes can you see in these flags?

There are squares in these flags.

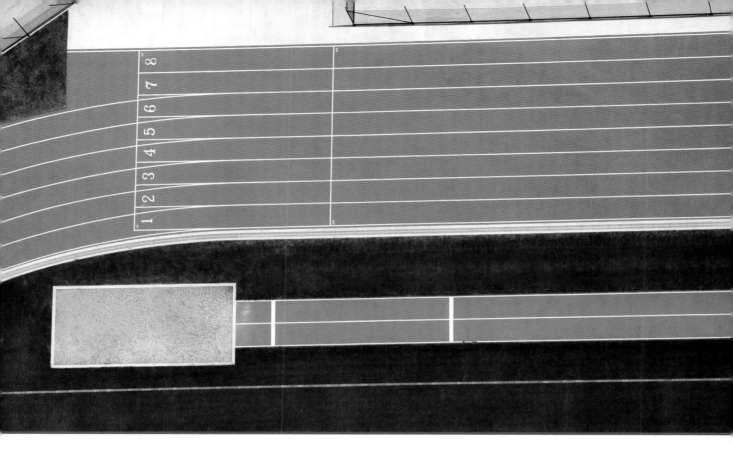

What shape is this sandpit?

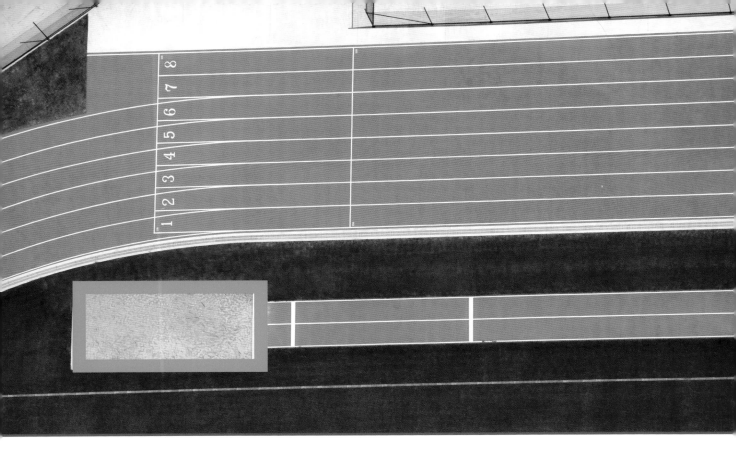

This sandpit is a rectangle.

What shape is this ball?

This ball is an oval.

What shape is this person making?

This person is making a triangle.

What shape is this kayak?

This kayak is a diamond.

What shape is on this ice?

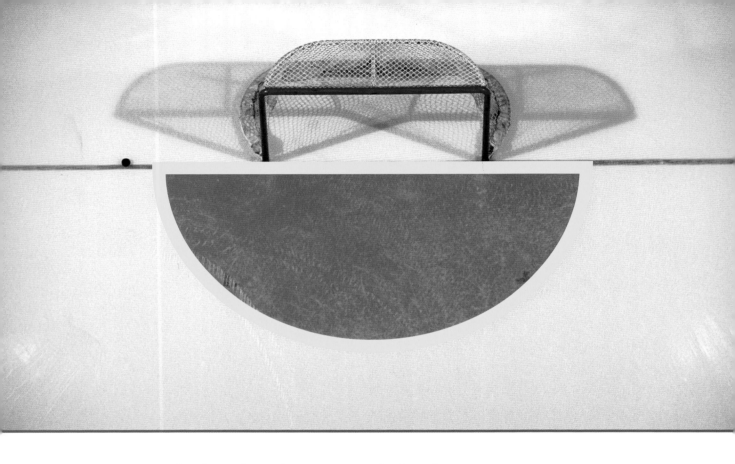

A semicircle is on this ice.

What shape are the wheels on this bike?

The wheels on this bike are circles.

There are many shapes in sport.
What shapes can you see?

Naming shapes

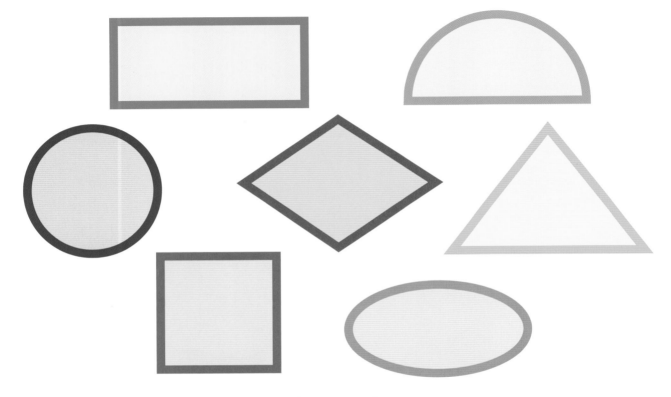

Can you remember the names of these shapes?